Disney

PIRATES of the CARIBBEAN
DEAD MAN'S CHEST

The Search for Dead Man's Chest

Adapted by Tisha Hamilton

Based on characters created by Ted Elliott & Terry Rossio
and Stuart Beattie and Jay Wolpert
Written by Ted Elliott & Terry Rossio
Based on Walt Disney's Pirates of the Caribbean
Produced by Jerry Bruckheimer
Directed by Gore Verbinski

Part One

Reader's Digest
Children's Books®

Pleasantville, New York • Montréal, Québec • Bath, United Kingdom

I t was a dark night as the notorious pirate ship, the *Black Pearl,* bobbed soundlessly on the ink-black ocean water. In the distance, its crew watched the looming stone towers of a foreign prison. Then a line of guards appeared, carrying long wooden boxes, each about the size and shape of a man. Coffins!

Splash! Crash! The still night was broken as, one by one, the boxes were dumped into the sea.

The prison guards were long gone when a sudden shotgun blast blew through the lid of one of the floating coffins. Soon a filthy hand emerged from the hole to fumble with the coffin latch. The lid creaked open, and Captain Jack Sparrow sat up.

He rummaged in the coffin for his hat. Then there was a cracking sound as he murmured, "Sorry, mate." With that, he pulled up a human leg bone and used it to paddle the coffin as if it were a canoe.

DISK 1
(1)

(2)

As his crew helped him aboard the *Black Pearl*, Jack revealed a long strip of cloth he had hidden in his sleeve. It bore a large drawing of a key — nothing more. What could it mean?

All Jack would say was that they had to find the key that matched the drawing. Then he took out his Compass, but he didn't seem to be able to get a reading from it. He flung out one arm and pointed. "Snap to, you ricket-ridden leeches!" he shouted. "I'll plot our course later."

The pirates grumbled as they set to their tasks. Setting sail without a heading was unheard of. What was Jack Sparrow thinking?

Meanwhile, Jack's cohorts from his last adventure on *Isla de Muerta* were having their own troubles. Elizabeth Swann and Will Turner had planned to be married. Instead, Lord Beckett and his men held them prisoner, accusing them of helping the convicted pirate, Jack Sparrow, escape.

④ Beckett ran the powerful East India Trading Company. A greedy schemer, he offered Will Turner a deal.

"These Letters of Marque amount to a full pardon for your pirate friend," Beckett said. In order to set Elizabeth free, Will had to trade the letters for Jack's Compass. Will didn't trust Beckett but he didn't have much choice.

Meanwhile, aboard the *Black Pearl,* Jack Sparrow was having a tough time. His Compass wasn't working, and the ship had been sailing aimlessly in the vast, dark ocean. Even so, Jack couldn't help sneaking peeks at the Compass. He kept hoping it would

DISK 2
①

show him something different. It never did, though, and every time he looked, he couldn't help also seeing the scar on his wrist. It was in the shape of the letter P, for pirate, and it had been branded there by none other than the nasty Lord Beckett.

Now it was late. The men of the *Black Pearl* were all asleep—all except Jack, that is. Suddenly, he sensed a visitor.

"Time's run out, Jack," an eerie voice whispered.

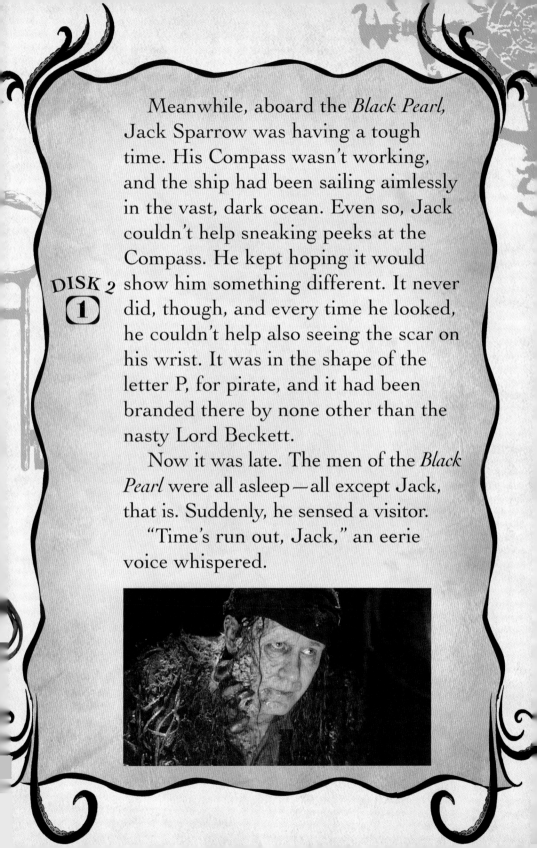

Jack knew that voice. Slowly, he turned to face a ghostly figure on the shadowy deck. Its face was as pale as a sun-bleached shell. Starfish and barnacles encrusted its face and body.

②   "Bootstrap?" Jack said, as he saw that it was Will Turner's father. "Bill Turner?"

Bootstrap had been sent by Davy Jones, the captain of the *Flying Dutchman*. There wasn't a sailor in all the world's oceans who didn't fear Davy Jones—with good reason. He collected many men in the cold, deep sea. On his *Flying Dutchman*, though, there was a fate worse than death. Davy Jones knew how to trick desperate men into serving as his crew, and then torment them endlesssly. Will's father had become one of these men.

"You made a deal with him, too, Jack,"
Bootstrap reminded him. "He raised the *Pearl*
from the depths for you, and thirteen years
you've been her Captain. The terms
that applied to me apply to you. One soul,
bound to crew a lifetime upon his ship."

"The *Flying Dutchman* already has a captain,"
Jack pointed out. "There's no need for me."

"Then it's the Locker for you," Bootstrap said
ominously. "Jones's Leviathan will find you and
drag the *Pearl* back to the depths, and you with
it. Your time is up." He pointed toward Jack's
hand, where a terrifying black spot suddenly
appeared. Jack yelped
and ran, but
Bootstrap had
disappeared.

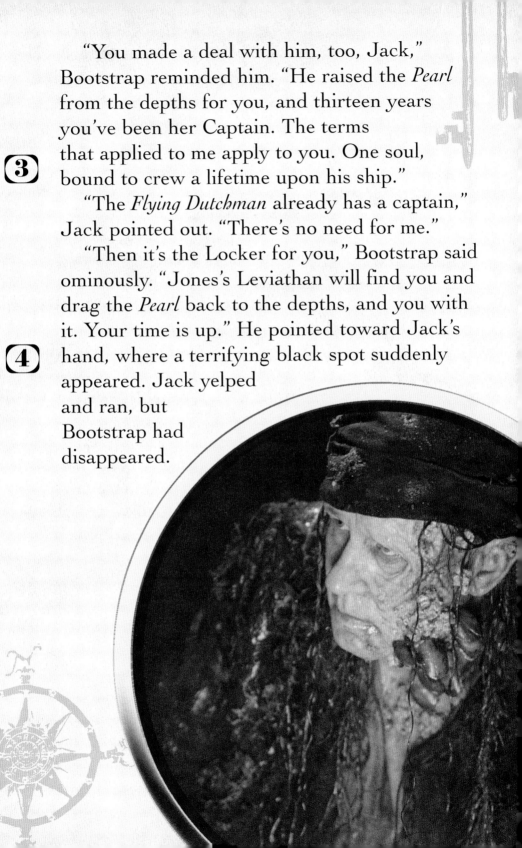

Meanwhile, Will Turner had set out on his journey to find Jack, but it wasn't easy. Everyone told him something different. He didn't know that Elizabeth had already managed to get free, and was on his trail.

DISK 3
①

With her father's help, Elizabeth had broken out of prison. Then, she had held Beckett at gunpoint to get the Letters of Marque. Now, she could use them to get pardons for all three of them—herself, Will, and Jack. But she had to find them first. Disguised as a sailor, she hid aboard a ship and tricked its crew into heading for Tortuga.

②

When Will finally found the *Black Pearl*, he could hardly believe his eyes. The empty ship lay in the sand where it had been beached on a tiny island. Jack had figured he'd be safe from Davy Jones as long as he stayed on land. What Bootstrap had told him had scared him clean out of the water.

Now it was time to leave the island. Jack looked at his useless Compass. He still hoped to outrun Davy Jones. The pirates pushed the *Pearl* off the beach. "Keep to the shallows!" he yelled. "Go anywhere, except where it might make sense for us to go!"

No one knew what he meant by that. All Will cared about was being reunited with Elizabeth. Now that he had found Jack, and was aboard the *Black Pearl,* he could get the Compass and save Elizabeth.

He spoke up, "I need that Compass, Jack." When Jack wouldn't hand it over, Will had no choice. Soon his sword was at Jack's throat.

"Hand it over. Now," he said.

Then Jack Sparrow did what he did best. He resorted to trickery.

He offered to trade Will the Compass if Will would find the key on the strip of fabric. That's how Will found himself paddling upriver in a longboat, headed toward the eerie shack belonging to Tia Dalma. Jack followed close behind in a second longboat.

3

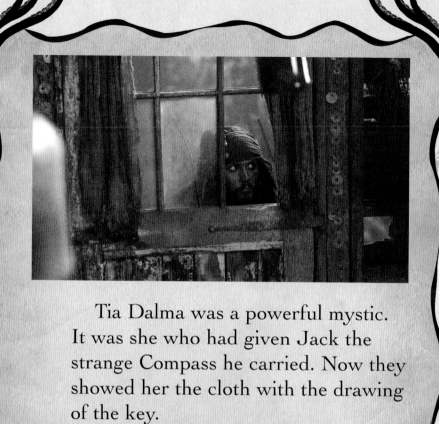

Tia Dalma was a powerful mystic. It was she who had given Jack the strange Compass he carried. Now they showed her the cloth with the drawing of the key.

"The key goes to a chest," she said. Then she told them the terrible story of Davy Jones, the captain of the *Flying Dutchman*. He was doomed to roam the seas forever, never setting foot on land. Long ago, his heart had been broken, and it hurt him so much that he vowed to live without it. He had carved his still-beating heart from his body. That's what he kept in the chest. "He keeps it with him at all times," she said, pointing at a drawing of the key.

Jack stood up briskly. "So all that's left is to slip aboard the *Flying Dutchman* and take the key."

"Let me see your hand," Tia Dalma said.

She looked at the Black Spot on Jack's hand. Then she gave him a jar filled with dirt.

"Land is where you are safe, Jack Sparrow, so you will carry land with you." Jack quickly returned to his ship and set sail.

The *Black Pearl*, a black ship with black sails, was invisible as it approached a scuttled ship. Soundlessly, Will climbed into a longboat and rowed toward it. Once on board, Will realized he had been tricked. This was not the *Flying Dutchman*! Just then, the true *Dutchman* appeared.

The unearthly ship seemed to be made of ancient driftwood, old bones, and barnacles. A human skull adorned its prow. Davy Jones himself seemed to be a creature of the sea, with his curling, living beard of octopus tentacles, and a claw in place of a missing arm.

His crewmen were equally strange. Some had scales or seaweed instead of skin while others had turned into coral and shell.

Jack watched Will from a safe distance aboard the *Black Pearl*. Will bravely faced the fearsome Davy Jones. He said what Jack had told him to, "Jack Sparrow sent me to settle his debt."

③   Davy Jones's face darkened to the shade of squid ink, and his tentacle beard waved dangerously. Then, to Jack Sparrow's horror, Davy Jones suddenly appeared aboard the *Black Pearl*. Jack Sparrow talked fast to save his own skin.

In the end, Davy Jones insisted that Will stay on his ship to serve with his ghoulish crew. In addition, Jack would have to find 99 other poor souls in three days' time. As Davy Jones vanished, so did the Black Spot on Jack's hand.

Back on the *Flying Dutchman*, Will came face to face with his long-lost father. He was upset to see that Bootstrap Bill was growing less human every day. On *Isla de Muerta*, Will thought he'd freed his father from the curse of the *Black Pearl* and a life of undying agony at the bottom of the ocean. He was dismayed to learn that his father had only traded one misery for another and was now doomed to serve out the same fate aboard the *Flying Dutchman*.

And for Bootstrap, the sight of his son after so many long years awakened his human feelings. He couldn't bear that Will now seemed doomed to the same cruel fate he was. But was there a way off the *Flying Dutchman*?

Meanwhile, Jack needed to find 99 sailors to pay his debt to Davy Jones. The *Black Pearl* docked in Tortuga to recruit more pirates. That's where Jack met up with Elizabeth—and his old adversary, Norrington.

Norrington had fallen on hard times after he'd lost Jack on *Isla de Muerta*. Ruined and desperate, he agreed to serve on the *Black Pearl*.

Jack tried to charm his way out of trouble with Elizabeth, but she brushed off his excuses and explanations. "All I want is to find Will," she said.

That gave Jack an idea. He had learned that the strange Compass he'd gotten from Tia Dalma wouldn't work because of the curse placed on him by Davy Jones. But Jack knew that Elizabeth was free of any curse so the Compass would work for her.

Jack persuaded Elizabeth to believe that finding Davy Jones's chest would lead her to Will.

As Elizabeth took the Compass, its needle moved back and forth, then pointed straight. The *Black Pearl* set sail, headed for the chest that held the still-beating heart of Davy Jones.

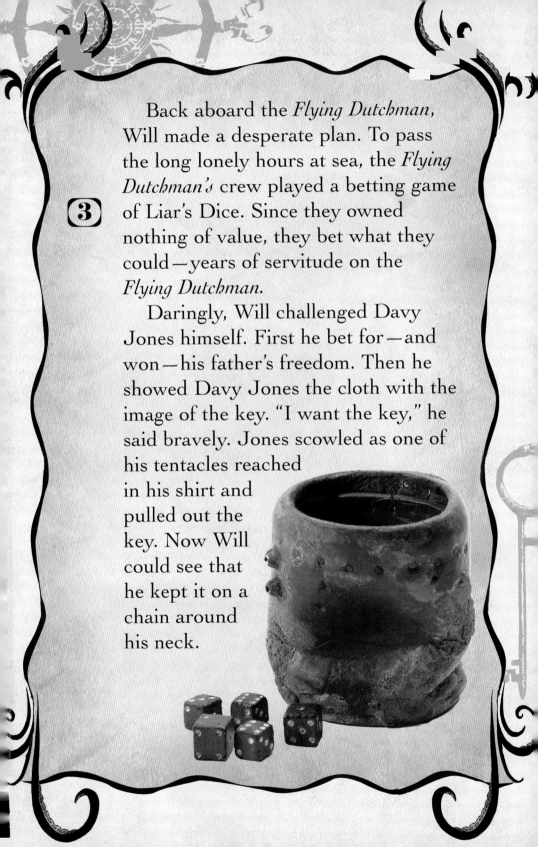

Back aboard the *Flying Dutchman*, Will made a desperate plan. To pass the long lonely hours at sea, the *Flying Dutchman's* crew played a betting game **3** of Liar's Dice. Since they owned nothing of value, they bet what they could—years of servitude on the *Flying Dutchman*.

Daringly, Will challenged Davy Jones himself. First he bet for—and won—his father's freedom. Then he showed Davy Jones the cloth with the image of the key. "I want the key," he said bravely. Jones scowled as one of his tentacles reached in his shirt and pulled out the key. Now Will could see that he kept it on a chain around his neck.

Will and Davy Jones began a new game. Will was winning, too, until Bootstrap unknowingly spoiled his plan by joining the game.

Bootstrap couldn't bear the idea of his son serving out his sentence aboard the *Flying Dutchman*. He made his bet—and lost. Now instead of Will winning the key and his father's freedom, both had been lost. Will was touched by his father's sacrifice, but he still needed that key. How could he get it now?

(4)

...continued in Part Two